For Ruby and Xavier—*JR*

Published by
MAGINATION PRESS®
American Psychological Association
750 First Street NE
Washington, DC 20002

Magination Press is a registered trademark of the American Psychological Association.

For more information about our books, including a complete catalog, please write to us, call 1-800-374-2721, or visit our website at www.apa.org/pubs/magination.

Book design by Susan K. White
Printed by Lake Book Manufacturing, Inc., Melrose Park, IL

Library of Congress Cataloging-in-Publication Data
Names: Rooks, Jo, author.
Title: A box of butterflies / Jo Rooks.
Description: Washington, DC : Magination Press, [2018]
Identifiers: LCCN 2017034413 | ISBN 9781433828713 (hardcover) |
   ISBN 1433828715 (hardcover)
Subjects: LCSH: Emotions in children—Juvenile literature. | Emotions—Juvenile literature.
Classification: LCC BF723.E6 R659 2018 | DDC 155.4/124—dc23 LC record available at
   https://lccn.loc.gov/2017034413

Manufactured in the United States of America
10 9 8 7 6 5 4 3 2

a box of Butterflies

Jo Rooks

MAGINATION PRESS 🦋 WASHINGTON, DC

American Psychological Association

"…and they all lived happily ever after. The end," said Robot.

"I love that story," said Ruby. "Did you love it too?"

"Robot is just a machine. Robot cannot feel love."

Robot paused for a moment and said,
"What does love feel like?"

Ruby replied, *"Love feels…"*

"…like a box of butterflies."

"…like a colorful dancing kite!"

"...like drinking in a sunset."

"...like a firefly in the night."

"Where does love come from?" asked Robot.

"It comes from inside," said Ruby.

"I can't see anything," said Robot.

"You can't see it. Only *feel* it!"
said Ruby.

"It's an emotion. You might feel
other ones, too."

"One is green and spiky like a twisted thistle.

Jealousy

X-BOT

I sometimes feel that way
when my best friend plays with
someone else."

"One is hot like a coal on the fire and smokes up through your head like a volcano.

ANGER

I sometimes feel that way when I'm told

NO MORE TV!"

"One is cold like a heavy stone
pressing on your tummy.

FEAR

I sometimes feel that
way when the lights
go out at night."

"One is like a little fly
that buzzes around your head
and sits on your nose.

WORRY

I sometimes feel
that way when I can't find my
special blanket."

"One is like
raindrops falling from
a big blue cloud.

Sadness

I sometimes feel that way on the last day of our vacation."

"Those don't sound so nice," said Robot.

"It's okay, Robot. Those feelings come and go just like happy ones. Everyone feels them sometimes," she said, and gently hugged him.

Then something began to happen…
something that had never happened
to Robot before!

Robot began to *feel* something…

something *fluttery*,

something *uplifting*,

something *warm*,

something *glowing* inside him…

...Love

Note to Parents & Caregivers

by Elizabeth McCallum, PhD

A Box of Butterflies is a charming story about a little girl teaching her friend Robot about all the emotions she sometimes feels and the situations that bring them about. Reading this book with your child can be a way to discuss feelings they may experience similar to the girl in the story. In discussing these various emotions, your child may be encouraged to engage in conversations about recognizing and managing their own emotions, and tools and strategies for doing so.

Why Are Emotions Important?

Human beings grow and develop quickly during childhood and adolescence. In addition to the obvious physical changes during these years, children are also developing at a rapid pace emotionally, socially, and intellectually. Emotional development includes understanding what emotions are, what brings them about, and recognizing feelings in oneself and others. In *A Box of Butterflies*, Ruby has a solid understanding of her own emotions and what situations lead to each feeling. She also has a well-developed sense of empathy, as evidenced by her eagerness to share her emotional knowledge with her friend Robot and her pleasure at his happiness when he feels the emotion love at the conclusion of the story.

Emotional development is a dynamic process that begins in infancy and continues into adulthood, with children developing more advanced emotions and strategies for managing them as they grow. The earliest emotions exhibited by babies include happiness, anger, sadness, and fear. As they grow older, additional emotions emerge including embarrassment, shyness, shame, guilt, and empathy. With age, their strategies for managing their emotions become more sophisticated, leading children to develop emotional skills that can serve them well throughout their life.

Important Emotional Skills

Research in the area of emotional development has consistently found some skills to be associated with a variety of positive outcomes including strong social relationships, high self-esteem, and overall happiness. Three of these important skills are *self-regulation, emotional self-awareness,* and *the ability to identify emotions in others.*

- **Self-regulation** is the ability to monitor and manage one's own emotional state and behavior. If I am feeling anxious, I can think about what stressors may be causing my anxiety and I can take steps to reduce the feeling, or I can change the situation that is causing the feeling, or both. For example, if I am experiencing physiological symptoms of anxiety (sweating, increased heartbeat, rapid breathing, etc.), I can stop and think about the anxiety being caused by an upcoming exam that I have not yet studied for. In this situation, I can relieve the anxious feelings by studying, or by practicing relaxation techniques such as meditation or yoga.

- **Emotional self-awareness** is the ability to understand one's own emotions and how they impact one's behavior. For example, an emotionally self-aware child may recognize that when they feel excited, they tend to become more talkative, and when they feel sad, they often go to their room and withdraw from family interaction. This knowledge allows them to reliably predict how they will respond to certain environmental circumstances.
- **Identifying emotions in others** has been shown to be linked to more success across a variety of domains, including social relationships, academics, and the workforce. Individuals with this ability tend to be more empathic and better able to take the perspectives of others who are different from themselves.

These emotional skills develop differently in each child. Some children may have strong emotional skills at a young age while others may take longer to develop these skills. The rate of emotional skill development can depend on a variety of factors including cultural differences and individual temperament, among others. For instance, some families and cultures emphasize the expression of a wide range of emotions, whereas others encourage children to be more reserved in their emotional expression, leading to measureable differences in emotional development cross-culturally.

Developing Strong Emotional Skills

Regardless of the developmental level of your child's emotional skills, parents and caregivers can help children in this process by using a variety of evidence-based strategies.

- **Learn to recognize your child's emotional responses.** It will be easy to identify some of your child's emotions (like joy and anger) while others may be less obvious (like shame, guilt, or embarrassment). Particularly when your child's emotions are hidden, it is important to pay attention to their words, body language, and behavior to offer clues as to how they may be feeling.
- **Help your child learn to identify their own emotional responses**. When you notice your child seems to be feeling a particular emotion, help them label the emotion and discuss possible events that may have contributed to that feeling. This will help them learn to predict the types of situations and events that are linked to certain emotional reactions in themselves.
- **Help your child develop empathy.** You can promote empathy by talking to your child about how others in distress (whether in real life, books, movies, TV,

etc.) may be feeling. Another way to encourage empathy is to help children see what they have in common with others. Meeting and learning about people from diverse backgrounds has been shown to increase empathy and overall emotional skills.

- **Model appropriate emotional skills.** Demonstrate appropriate emotional skills and discuss how you manage your emotions even when it is difficult. For example, when someone cuts in front of you with your child in line at the supermarket, take a moment to discuss the importance of keeping one's cool in a frustrating situation.

Emotional development is a process that begins in infancy and continues into adulthood. Parents and caregivers can help children to develop a variety of strategies to help them become emotionally skilled individuals who are able to self-regulate and manage their own emotions in a complex and challenging world. While individual children develop at different rates, most children's emotional skills fall within a range of typical development. However, if you have concerns about your child's emotional development, you should discuss these concerns with your pediatrician or a mental health professional.

Elizabeth McCallum, PhD, is an associate professor in the school psychology program at Duquesne University, as well as a Pennsylvania certified school psychologist. She is the author of many scholarly journal articles and book chapters on topics including academic and behavioral interventions for children and adolescents.

About the Author & Illustrator

Jo Rooks is an illustrator, author, and graphic designer living in leafy South West London with her husband and two children. Jo studied at Bath School of Art and Design and pursued a career in graphic design. When Jo had her two children, she began to rediscover her love of art, poetry, and creative writing for children. She is passionate about reading with children and hopes to bring lovable characters and meaningful messages in her story books.

About Magination Press

Magination Press is an imprint of the American Psychological Association, the largest scientific and professional organization representing psychologists in the United States and the largest association of psychologists worldwide.